A Note to Parents and Caregivers:

Read-it! Readers are for children who are just starting on the amazing road to reading. These beautiful books support both the acquisition of reading skills and the love of books.

The RED LEVEL presents familiar topics using common words and repeating sentence patterns.
The BLUE LEVEL presents new ideas using a larger vocabulary and varied sentence structure.
The YELLOW LEVEL presents more challenging ideas, a broad vocabulary, and wide variety in sentence structure.

When sharing a book with your child, read in short stretches, pausing often to talk about the pictures. Have your child turn the pages and point to the pictures and familiar words. And be sure to reread favorite stories or parts of stories.

There is no right or wrong way to share books with children. Find time to read with your child and pass on the legacy of literacy.

Adria F. Klein, Ph.D.
Professor Emeritus
California State University
San Bernardino, California

First American edition published in 2003 by
Picture Window Books
5115 Excelsior Boulevard
Suite 232
Minneapolis, MN 55416
1-877-845-8392
www.picturewindowbooks.com

First published in Great Britain by Franklin Watts, 96 Leonard Street, London, EC2A 4XD
Text © Susan Gates 2000
Illustration © Anni Axworthy 2000

Printed in the United States of America.
1 2 3 4 5 6 08 07 06 05 04 03

Library of Congress Cataloging-in-Publication Data
Gates, Susan.
  Bill's baggy pants / written by Susan Gates ; illustrated by Anni Axworthy.—1st American ed.
    p. cm. — (Read-it! readers)
  Summary: Bill is very proud of his new baggy pants with the many pockets but when he goes to buy potatoes for his mother, strange things begin to happen.
  ISBN 1-4048-0050-6
  [1. Pants---Fiction. 2. Blacks---England---Fiction. 3. Humorous stories.] I. Axworthy, Anni; ill. II. Title. III.
Series.
  PZ7.G2234 Bi 2003
  [E]---dc21   2002074946

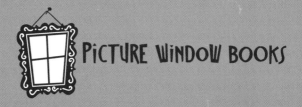

Read-it! Readers
Red Level

Bill's Baggy Pants

Written by Susan Gates

Illustrated by Anni Axworthy

Reading Advisors:
Adria F. Klein, Ph.D.
Professor Emeritus, California State University
San Bernardino, California

Picture Window Books
Minneapolis, Minnesota

Bill's mom bought him
some new pants.

The pants were very
big and baggy.

They had lots of pockets.

Bill's mom sent him to the store.

"I can put the groceries
in my pockets," said Bill.

"I'd like some potatoes, please," said Bill to the shopkeeper.

11

The shopkeeper helped
Bill fill his pockets with
the potatoes.

"I can't walk!" said Bill.

"My pants are much

too heavy."

Bill took all the potatoes
out of his pockets.

Suddenly, the wind began
to blow up Bill's pants.

They got bigger and
bigger and bigger.

Bill floated high up into the sky.

21

He floated over the town

and waved to his mom
n the yard.

23

Bill's mom didn't see him.

24

"Look at me, Mom!"
shouted Bill.

Suddenly, a bird pecked
Bill's pants.

hey went *sssssssssss!*

Bill's pants got
smaller and smaller.

"Look out! I'm coming down," he shouted.

Bill landed next to his mom in the yard.

"You got home quickly!"
she said.

Red Level

The Best Snowman, by Margaret Nash 1-4048-0048-4
Bill's Baggy Pants, by Susan Gates 1-4048-0050-6
Cleo and Leo, by Anne Cassidy 1-4048-0049-2
Felix on the Move, by Maeve Friel 1-4048-0055-7
Jasper and Jess, by Anne Cassidy 1-4048-0061-1
The Lazy Scarecrow, by Jillian Powell 1-4048-0062-X
Little Joe's Big Race, by Andy Blackford 1-4048-0063-8
The Little Star, by Deborah Nash 1-4048-0065-4
The Naughty Puppy, by Jillian Powell 1-4048-0067-0
Selfish Sophie, by Damian Kelleher 1-4048-0069-7

Blue Level

The Bossy Rooster, by Margaret Nash 1-4048-0051-4
Jack's Party, by Ann Bryant 1-4048-0060-3
Little Red Riding Hood, by Maggie Moore 1-4048-0064-6
Recycled!, by Jillian Powell 1-4048-0068-9
The Sassy Monkey, by Anne Cassidy 1-4048-0058-1
The Three Little Pigs, by Maggie Moore 1-4048-0071-9

Yellow Level

Cinderella, by Barrie Wade 1-4048-0052-2
The Crying Princess, by Anne Cassidy 1-4048-0053-0
Eight Enormous Elephants, by Penny Dolan 1-4048-0054-9
Freddie's Fears, by Hilary Robinson 1-4048-0056-5
Goldilocks and the Three Bears, by Barrie Wade 1-4048-0057-3
Mary and the Fairy, by Penny Dolan 1-4048-0066-2
Jack and the Beanstalk, by Maggie Moore 1-4048-0059-X
The Three Billy Goats Gruff, by Barrie Wade 1-4048-0070-0